At School

Written by Roderick Hunt and Annemarie Young

Illustrated by Alex Brychta

OXFORD
UNIVERSITY PRESS

Kipper was excited. It was his first day at school.

He was feeling a bit scared too, so he wanted to take Little Ted. "All right," said Mum, "but don't forget your book bag."

Mum went to the classroom with
Kipper. He was glad that his new
friend Anna was there. A helper
called Trish met them at the door.

Trish showed Kipper his peg.
It had his name above it, and his
picture was underneath. Kipper put
his bag on his peg.

Then Trish showed Anna and
Kipper a special box. "Put your toys
in here," she said. "They'll be safe."

But Kipper didn't want to put
Little Ted in the box. He went back
to his peg and put Ted in his bag.

Kipper's teacher was Miss Green.
"It's time to begin," she said, so Mum
said goodbye to Kipper.

Kipper was worried. "You will
come back for me?" he asked.

"Of course I will," said Mum.
"Don't worry."

Miss Green took the register, and
then they all sang a song.

Then Miss Green said, "We're
going to look around the school now."

Kipper wanted Little Ted to look around the school too.

"You can show him around after school," said Miss Green.

"Here are the toilets," said Miss
Green. "If you need to go, don't
wait, or it may be too late."

Then Miss Green showed them the hall. Biff and Chip were doing PE.

"We have assembly in here, and lunch as well," she said.

Playtime was fun. All the children wanted to play on the logs.

"Take it in turns," said Miss Green.

Kipper wanted to get Ted, but
Anna called him. "Come and play,"
she said.

After play, the children did a
drawing. Anna drew her lamb.
Kipper drew a picture of Ted.

"Can I get Ted now?" asked Kipper.

"You can get Ted after school,"
said Trish. "We're going to do hand
prints now."

Kipper made three green
handprints. Anna made a red one.
   "Can I show Ted?" asked Kipper.
   "Soon," said Trish, "after school."

Anna's nose was itchy, so she
rubbed her face. Now she had paint
on her nose! Miss Green cleaned it
off, but Anna was a bit upset.

Then Kipper and the other children made Anna laugh, so she wasn't upset anymore.

Soon it was time to go home. "I can show my pictures to Ted now," said Kipper. He looked in his bag, but Ted wasn't there!

Kipper began to cry. "I've lost Little Ted," he said.

"Don't worry," said Trish. "We'll find him."

Just then, Anna put her hand in her bag. "Look! Here's Ted," she said. "You put him in my bag!"

Mum and Dad came to get Kipper.
"Did you have fun?" asked Dad.
"Yes," said Kipper, "but I'm going
to leave Ted at home tomorrow."

Talk about the story

Where *should* Kipper have put Little Ted?

What do you think Kipper said when Anna found Little Ted?

What else do you think Kipper could do at school?

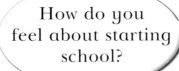

How do you feel about starting school?

At school

Talk about the things that happen at school.
Which things did Kipper and Anna do on their first day?

the register

computer

sand play

lunch time

dressing up

counting

storytime

playtime

singing a song

reading

A Maze

Help Kipper find Little Ted.